ORDER FROM

CHILDREN'S PRESS, INC.

CHICAGO, ILL.

PUBLISHERS

D1283099

TELEPHONE WIRES UP!

by RUTH TOOZE

illustrated by

William Hutchinson

MELMONT PUBLISHERS, Inc., Chicago

New Everyday Adventure Stories serve through exciting tales to acquaint a young reader with the people who serve a community and with the work they do.

An easy-to-read story, valuable in social studies for family relations and the study of communication.

Further information about telephone workers will be found in the appendix at the back of this book.

Previously published under the title of
Wires Up!
Copyright 1952, by Julian Messner, Inc.

Revised edition published, 1964, by Melmont Publishers, Inc.
Printed in the U.S.A.
Published simultaneously in Canada

Library of Congress Catalog Card Number: 64-16792

About this Story

The Martin family have fun together with their latest hobby, bird watching. Just when John and his father are thrilled over their bird feeder, Mr. Martin has to leave for Brazil. He hopes he will be back by the time the purple martins arrive for their convention in late March. John is unhappy about the trip, but Dad points to the telephone wires in back of their house and says he will never be farther away than those wires, so long as they are up.

John watches the birds and records them in his book. He has many calls from his dad. He celebrates a birthday and he works on a communications project for school, listing all the ways a telephone is useful. Just as John is expecting an important call from his dad, the purple martins arrive. Hundreds of them settle on the telephone wires and their weight breaks the wires. But the trouble man comes and repairs them just in time for the call to come through. All wires are up! The purple martins' convention is over—the Martin family reunion is about to begin.

JOHN tiptoed down the stairs to the dining-room window early in the morning on the day after Christmas. The new bird feeder was still there. He pulled on his boots, put on his coat and took a cup of seeds and fresh piece of suet out to the feeder. He sprinkled some of the seeds on top of the glass and around it on the snow to help birds find the feeder. A big, saucy blue jay flew down so fast, he almost pecked John's hand as he was fixing the suet in its holder. By the time John got back into the house the Martin family were down for breakfast.

"Did you see that jay? I hope he doesn't keep the other birds away."

"He won't," answered dad. "That is part of the reason for the glass, to give small birds a chance."

After breakfast John and his father stood at the window looking at their new bird feeder, a gift from Aunt Alice. The Martin family had fun doing things together. They had several hobbies. The one they loved the best was bird watching. "What fun we are going to have with this new feeder, especially dad and I," John was thinking.

"Look, dad, the cardinals have found it."

"There's a nuthatch coming down the tree," said dad.

"We'll get every bird that stays around here in winter," answered John, who got more and more excited as new birds appeared.

"Son," said Mr. Martin.

John looked up quickly. His father only called him 'Son' when he had something special to tell him or was going to scold him.

"Son, I have to make another trip. I'm leaving the end of the week for Brazil."

"Oh dad, not now, not just when we were going to see more birds than we've ever seen."

John loved his family but especially his father. They were the men of the family and had special fun of their own. Only one thing was wrong with the family. Dad was an engineer and worked for a company that did business all over the world, so he often had to go away on long trips. Dad always joked about it and said, "All Martins have itchy feet, John. You will, too." He meant that all Martins liked to go places. Aunt Alice travelled for the conservation bureau talking about birds and trees and soil. Uncle Jim was a mining engineer and travelled to many far countries.

The travelling Martins!

Right now John did not want his father to go away. Mother came over to the window and dad turned Janie's high chair around so she could see, too.

"Oh dad, of all times for you to have to go away," John began again. "Is it a long trip?"

"Well, not as long as it could be. I'm going to South America. I think I'll be in Rio most of the time. Rio de Janeiro is in Brazil. I'll fly both ways. I think I can be back in about three months. I might get here for the martins' convention."

This was a family joke. Well, not quite a joke, one of those special family possessions. Every year between March twenty-seventh and March thirtieth, the purple martins came. On their way north, they stopped in Wilmette, Illinois, where the John

9

Martins lived. Always on one of these March days,
when the winds blew and winter gray clouds were
turning to white clouds, they came. Hundreds and
hundreds of them. They lit on the telephone wires
out in back and sat there crowded close together,
fluttering and chattering for most of the day. One
or two birds flew up and down the lines as if check-

ing. Those checkers sometimes stopped near the
middle and sat on that long branch of the oak tree
and talked. It was a lecture. You could tell it was.
The chattering and fluttering all died down. Those
birds listened. When the leader bird was through,
the chatter, chatter, chatter began again, just like a
convention of people. The martins' convention.

The Martin family felt it belonged to them just as if the birds knew this was a Martin home. There were always hundreds more on their wires than on any of the neighbors' wires.

Every year, too, some martins stayed behind and nested. John and his father had put up many bird houses in their back yard. Quite a few of the martins moved in and stayed to raise their families.

"Dad, I wish you didn't have to go so far. You never went so far before, did you?"

"Yes, the trip to India was much farther. But you weren't big enough to mind that time. Look, John. See our telephone wires out there? I'm really never any farther away than that wire. I can always get to some place where there is a telephone and talk to you. That wire brings you my voice. It is our connecting wire."

"Even from Brazil, dad? Can you telephone to us?"

"Sure I can, Johnny, and I will. It costs quite a lot of money because it is so far away and there are so many wires to connect both countries. But the wires are there and can always carry my voice to you. So I am really only as far away as that wire."

"A wire is kind of a special thing, isn't it, dad?"

"Yes, Johnny, every wire is good for some interesting use. A telephone wire is very special because now the whole world is connected as it never was before. A man named Bell discovered that he could send a voice along a wire from one place to another. But that's a long story, a very interesting one which you might like to read some day," answered dad.

John got so interested in a connecting wire that he almost forgot about his father's going away so soon.

"That gives me some good ideas, John. Want to know my first one?" Dad went to his desk and brought out a record sheet with the days listed across the top. Down the side were places to write in the names of birds. Lines across and lines up and down made squares.

"This is your bird record. We'll write down December twenty-sixth in this first date space. On the side we can put in blue jay, cardinal, nuthatch for today."

"Sparrows. They'll be there every day. Do we put

them in?" asked John, as he studied the chart.

"Well, they're birds, aren't they, even if there are a lot of them? If your record is going to be good, I'd put in all birds even if you don't like some of them," laughed dad.

"This will be fun. Have to add juncos now. Look, there are six of them in under the glass. I bet they like that protection while they eat." John wrote down the four kinds of birds, blue jay, cardinal, nuthatch, junco.

"I know you will have fun watching so many birds so closely with this feeder. It will be interesting to know how many birds do winter here. My!

15

but I'll be eager to see this record when I get back."

"You said you had another idea, dad," John reminded him.

"So I did. Birds won't take all your spare time," said dad with a twinkle in his eye. "Why don't you find out all the ways a family uses a telephone wire? Maybe your class at school would be interested."

"And how! This is funny, dad. It really is. We are studying communication in our grade right now."

John wasn't watching his father any more. He was looking at that telephone wire.

"I'll use it this minute."

John picked up the receiver and called his best friend Tim. When he hung up he asked, "What did people do to talk to their friends in other places before the telephone?"

"They didn't talk to them," his mother answered.

"I'm glad I didn't live then."

John took a sheet of paper, wrote TELE-PHONE at the top and put down—"Talking to your friends."

*　　*　　*

The next week flew like the wind. Sledding on their hill had never been so good. The police department closed their street to traffic so the children could coast while the snow was there.

Every morning John put out seed for the birds. Many birds came as soon as he put it out. He soon added chickadees and starlings to his list. Some days he counted over fifty birds in and around the feeder. He liked to watch the small birds, especially the nuthatch as he came head first down the trunk of the oak tree. One morning there was another small grayish bird with a little tuft on his head. "That's not a nuthatch. Let's look it up."

It was easy to find in the bird book. It was a tufted titmouse.

"Never saw you before, you perky little fellow."

Dad left on New Year's Day. There was too much ice and snow on the roads to drive him all the way to the Chicago Airport. They just drove him to the hotel in Evanston where he took the airport bus. He telephoned them from New York that night. It sounded as if he were talking from the next room.

"You sound so close, dad," said John.

"I am close, as close as that wire. Remember?"

"You really are, dad," answered John.

"Next call will be from Rio where I shall be most of the time. Goodbye, John."

Three days later the telephone rang. "Long distance, mom," shouted John.

It was dad calling.

"Hi, my J's. I had a fine trip all the way. I'm in my hotel now."

"You sound as close as if you were in the next room, dad."

"Well, I am as close as the telephone wire."

"You really are, dad. Goodbye."

On the tenth of January, mother stopped to pick up John just as school was out at 3:30.

They went to town to shop and pay their telephone bill. While mother went to the paying window, she told John to look at the rack where there were several free booklets. They told about the telephone and how to use it. There was one large booklet with a picture of a kind-looking old man with a white beard. John could read, "Bell," his last name.

"Oh mom, this must be the story of the man who invented the telephone. It says, 'Bell.'"

"Alexander Graham Bell is his full name."

"I'll take one and you can read it to me tonight."

That night mother read John the story of the Bell family who moved from Scotland to Canada. Alexander Graham Bell was interested in sound and speech. He was also interested in electricity. He often did many experiments with tuning forks, bars of iron, coils of wire and batteries. He worked with his friend, Thomas Watson. One day Watson heard Bell's voice come over a wire from another room. They were so excited over their talking wire.

And that was the beginning of the telephone.
"What a man!" exclaimed John as mother finished. "I almost feel as if I knew him. And because
of him, it isn't so hard to have dad far away, is it?
I think our class would be interested in this. Right

now we're finding all the ways a family uses a tele-
phone. So far this is what we have—
   Talking to friends
   Talking to family in Chicago (or far away)
   Ordering groceries
   Ordering medicine
   Calling the doctor
   Calling the garage if your car won't start
   Making appointments to have your hair cut or

to go to the dentist

Calling up people about meetings

Calling up the railroad station and airport for information about when trains and planes start or arrive

Reporting a fire

Reporting a burglar to the police

Calling for help if something goes wrong

Sending a telegram

We decided it would be very hard to live without a telephone today. That man Bell was really wonderful."

February was a little warmer. Every day the birds came to the feeder, blue jays and cardinals; the little chicadees, nuthatches and titmice; the juncos and starlings and sparrows and more sparrows. One morning a large black crow appeared. After that more crows came. It was lucky they were too big to bother the little birds who went under the glass.

"That makes nine," said John one morning as he marked down the birds on his record. "Wish there were ten."

Just then he saw a strange bird, about the size of the starling but with lighter colors and a yellow band across the end of his tail feathers. He ran for the bird book.

"It's a cedar waxwing. The chart shows that it winters here. We never had one before." Two cedar waxwings came all that week, but after that John saw them only twice.

"I guess these ten birds are about all the birds there are that stay through the winter."

"I think we have the chief ones," answered mother. "We never saw all of these until we had this feeder. I'm glad Aunt Alice gave it to us."

"How I wish dad could see them all!"

"He can see your record when he gets home. He'll be so interested," said mother.

His friends, Tim and Ted, had feeders too, and kept track of the birds which came to them. There were few trees near Ted's house so he never had any nuthatches or titmice. Tim forgot to put out seed

every day so he did not have as many birds in his
record as John.

One morning they woke up to see a surprise
world outside. It wasn't snow, it wasn't rain. It was
ice all over everything—every blade of grass, every
weed and flower stalk, every needle of the fir trees,
every tiny twig and big branch of the trees, every
telephone wire. There had been a sleet storm in the
night. It was so beautiful. When the sun came out
later, the whole world shone like a fairy land.

The papers told about telephone wires breaking
from the ice in many cities in the middle west. John
watched their wires closely all day. The sun was not

very warm and did not melt the ice. The ice held
those wires stiff for two whole days. Aunt Alice was
coming to dinner that night but she never came and
she did not telephone. That was not like her. The
next day she telephoned from Springfield.

"I've been kept here," she said. "The roads are
sheets of ice. The ice broke telephone wires so I
couldn't talk to you, but all the wires are up again."

The wires up again!

"That's good," thought John. "I hope our wires
are never down, especially when dad is away." He
looked out of the window. Most of the ice was
gone. All their wires were up.

*   *   *

February twenty-third was John's birthday, the day after George Washington's birthday. He would be nine years old this year. His birthday would come on Saturday.

Mother suggested he ask five boys over for lunch and games in the basement play room.

"That's my idea of a real party. No girls."

Mother laughed. "Janie and I will be here."

"You're different. I mean no third grade girls."

The first thing Saturday morning the telephone rang. It was Grandmother saying "Happy Birthday." It rang again while they were at breakfast. It was Western Union calling John Prescott Martin, Jr.

"Here I am," answered John.

Someone started singing, "Happy Birthday to you, Happy Birthday to you, Happy Birthday dear John, Happy Birthday to you. Aunt Alice"

It was a singing telegram.

"It makes you feel sort of silly listening to it, but it's fun," said John as he hung up the receiver. The postman came about ten o'clock. He brought three packages. There were new ping pong rackets in one. There was a small bird book that fit into a pocket in another. The third had a book about Aleck Bell.

The telephone rang again. Another telegram. This one came from Uncle Jim in Mexico.

"HAPPY BIRTHDAY. KEEP ALL WIRES UP TILL
WE ALL COME HOME.

UNCLE JIM"

John ran to the window to look at his telephone
wires. They were all up. They had a lot to do with
his birthday and this was the first time he had ever
thought about them. If you belonged to a travelling family you were lucky to have connecting wires
up.

The boys all came promptly at twelve. Mother
served lunch right away down in the play room. No
fancy stuff. They liked that. They had hamburgers
in buns, with catsup and pickles, tomato and let-
tuce salad, potato chips, all on paper plates. Three
hamburgers apiece!

Then mother brought in mugs of hot chocolate with a marshmallow melting on top of each one and big dishes of vanilla ice cream. Grandmother came right behind her with a big round cake covered with chocolate frosting and nine lighted candles.

She put that down in front of John.

"Blow them out, John, and make a wish. It will

come true if you blow them all out in one blow,"
said George.

"And if you don't tell the wish," added Tim.

John waited a minute. He wished, "Bring dad
home soon," but he didn't tell anyone. Then he
blew hard. All the candles went out.

"I'm glad. Hope my wish comes true."

Soon there wasn't much cake left.

Mother said, "I'm going to let you work out your own games, boys."

George and Ted started the first ping pong game. John, Tim, Jerry and Dick played darts. Then there was parchesi. They took turns at everything.

When they went home around five o'clock, the boys said it was the best party they had ever had.

"We had a he-man lunch, no fancy party stuff. Thank you, Mrs. Martin," said Ted.

"Let's go upstairs and have our family presents now," said mother. Janie was up from her nap. Grandmother was still there.

"More? I thought my party was your present, mom. It was the best birthday party I ever went to. It was just right."

"This is from Janie and this from me," said mother as she handed him two more packages.

"And this is my happy birthday, John," said grandmother.

John sat down on the floor to open his packages. There was a cub scout knife from grandmother.

There was a tuning fork from Janie. There was a

battery, some wire and other electrical equipment in a box from mother.

"Now I can make some experiments, too. This is good! Thank you, thank you."

John was hitting the tuning fork. Janie was sitting on mother's lap watching him. She slid down and walked across to him, holding out her hands for the fork.

"Catch her, John," called mother.

Janie had never tried to take any steps alone before. Now she took several steps all at once. John held her with one hand. With the other hand he struck the fork again and she laughed and laughed.

"Well, Janie, that's an extra birthday present. Good girl!"

It was the best birthday John had ever had—except for one thing. Dad wasn't there. All day John had thought one of those telephone calls might be dad. John knew it was hard sometimes to get clear wires all the way.

Mother went to the kitchen to fix supper. John was tinkering with his coil of wire. The telephone bell rang.

"I'll get it," he called. "Long distance, mom. Better come."

Mother came running, but John talked first. He had so much to tell, he spoke very fast.

"Hi dad. Everything's fine. All the boys were here. I got your book. And mom gave me electrical stuff for experiments. I'm going to fix a talking wire.

"And dad, Janie walked. Just now she slid down from mom's lap and walked over to me where I was sounding a tuning fork. Come home soon. Here's mom."

John gave the receiver to his mother who finished the conversation.

"Now I've had everything," said John. "I guess you could call it a perfect birthday."

                    *   *   *

March blew in like a lion.

"Now it will go out like a lamb," John said to Tim. "That will be good for the martins' convention."

"You always get the most martins on your wire. I hope I see the first bluebird. Sometimes they get here in March if it's mild enough," Tim answered.

"Robins, too. I'm getting the first robin," Ted said. He hoped he would beat the other boys at one point in their bird watching.

But it stayed cold and windy most of the month. The same winter birds came to their feeders every day. John's record showed nine or ten kinds every day. Often there were as many as ten or fifteen of one kind, especially juncos.

Sunday morning, March twenty-second, the telephone rang at seven-thirty o'clock in the morning. No one in the Martin house was awake. It rang and rang.

"John, run and answer that call, please," mother said sleepily.

John ran to the telephone. It was Ted.

"There's a robin in our side yard, a big fat one. Any in yours? I bet I'm first," shouted Ted, in great excitement.

"Yes, you are. Good for you, Ted," answered John.

"What is it John?" called mother.

"Only a robin. I mean it's Ted. We're all watch-

ing for robins and bluebirds. A few come in March. Tim and I beat Ted in everything. We have more birds and more kinds and Ted wanted to see the first robin. I'm glad he did."

When John went out with the seed there was a robin right under his feeder. Down went the robin on his bird record.

The next day at school several children reported seeing a robin in their yards. But the early bird, Ted, saw the first one.

There was a long letter from dad when John got home from school. Dad said his business was just about finished. He thought he would be able to leave the twenty-seventh or twenty-eighth and reach New York the twenty-ninth or thirtieth. He hoped he would be just in time for the purple martins' convention and a family Martin reunion. Uncle Jim was due back from Mexico. Aunt Alice was to be in their part of the state that week. Dad said he would telephone from New York as soon as he landed.

John walked over to the window and stood looking at the wires. He felt those wires were his and dad's in a special way. The wires were up, swinging up and down gently in the soft evening wind.

The weather changed that week. The wind changed around to the south. It grew warmer. The twenty-seventh came—a mild gray day, but no martins. The twenty-eighth came. There was some wind. White clouds piled up in the sky. The children watched eagerly, morning, noon and night. No martins.

The twenty-ninth came. It was a clear, shining Sunday, with only a few white clouds near the horizon. There was almost no wind. Ted and Tim came over to play ping pong with John. Late in the afternoon they were looking for martins when Tim shouted, "Look!"

There was a bluebird right in the middle of the lawn, hopping nearer the bird feeder. Soon he flew right up on the feeder and began eating.

"You got your wish, Tim. You saw the first bluebird."

"But in your yard, not mine," said Tim.

"Just because you were here doesn't matter. You saw it," answered John.

The sun went down. Still no martins.

It was eight o'clock, time for bed and still no call from dad. John thought he would never go to sleep, but he did.

He ran to the window as soon as he was up next morning, but there were no martins. His wires swayed a little in the wind. Tim and Ted were calling out in front. So he joined them and went to school. School was out at two o'clock because of some special meeting for the teachers. The three boys started home together.

"Look! They're here," shouted John.

Sure enough, there were several purple martins up on the telephone wires. The boys ran straight to John's home. There they were, hundreds and hundreds, all crowded on the wires in back of the Martins' home. The boys just stood and looked. Now that the birds were really here there was nothing to say. The birds were making so much noise with their twittering, there was no use in boys talking.

One bird began to fly along the wires all the way from one end to the other. The noise died down. The birds crowded close together.

47

"Look John. That lower wire is sagging. There are too many birds on it," said Tim.

"Those wires can hold any number of birds. They're strong," answered John.

Then it happened in an instant.

The wire broke.

The birds flew up. The birds from other wires flew up. Soon they were flying off in all directions.

"Martins can hold their convention somewhere else on any wires," John shouted, "but this is Monday, March thirtieth and dad is probably landing in New York this very minute. Our wires are down and he can't reach us by telephone. We have to get them fixed right away."

John ran in to tell mother.

"Mr. Boyd is probably home, John. Go ask him to help you get the repair service at once. Dad may be landing this minute. Hurry, John," said mother.

John did not need to be told to hurry. Mr. Boyd lived the second house down. He was home and eager to help.

"The grocery store on Central Street is on an-

other circuit," he said as they climbed into his car
to drive over there quickly.

Repair Service said a trouble man would be out
soon.

When John returned home, Ted and Tim were
still there, but no martins.

"I hope they found a place for their convention,
and don't try to crowd too many on one wire
again," John said.

The boys watched anxiously for the green repair
wagon.

In less than an hour it was there, the dark green
auto with ladders on the sides. Two men jumped
down.

"It's hard to believe," said Tom, the tall one,

when the boys told them how the wire broke because too many birds crowded on· to it, "but it is broken. It's a clean break. The wire is still good so we can splice it."

They opened the doors to the wagon. Inside were big coils of wire on reels. There were tools on the sides.

"Hand me a sleeve, Jack," said Tom.

Jack handed Tom a small hollow piece of wire called a sleeve.

Tom cut the end of the wire back to the place where it was firm. He sand-papered the end of the wire and slipped it halfway into the sleeve to a dent. The sleeve was soft. Tom took a tool from his pocket and crimped the wire tight inside the sleeve.

Meanwhile, Jack put up a ladder. Ted helped him get it firm against the telephone pole. Jack found the other end of the wire, cut it back to the firm part and sand-papered that end. Then Tom climbed up, lifting the long span of wire with the splicing sleeve on the end. He held it securely so Jack could slip his wire into the other end as far as the dent. Tom crimped that end into the sleeve.

Then Jack wrapped the wire securely around the steel pins on the cross arms and replaced the glass cap insulator. He checked all the glass caps while he was up there.

"Wires up again," said Jack as he climbed down the ladder. The men let the boys help replace the ladder on the side of the repair auto.

They showed the boys all the tools inside, the big coils of wire, and answered all their questions. Tom even spliced a short piece of wire so they could see just how it worked and how secure it was when the wire was crimped into the sleeve. John told the men about his father and how they expected a telephone call any minute from New York.

"Our wires just have to be up. Dad thought he might get home for the martins' convention but he didn't make it," said John.

"We have to call from your telephone to be sure everything is all right and report that to our office," said Tom.

John brought Tom into the house and introduced him to his mother. Tom called the repair office, and got an answer at once. Then he told them what he had done and that everything was in order again.

"We are grateful to you for coming so quickly. We are expecting a call any minute from my husband who is just flying home from Brazil," said mother.

"Glad we could help," answered Tom. "It is important to have all wires up."

The green repair auto drove away.

"I wish we knew where the birds went. They need a resting place here before going on north," John said.

"Oh, they will find other wires. Birds know what to do," answered Ted.

Ted and Tim went on to their homes, feeling lucky over all this excitement on the afternoon there was no school. John went inside the house.

The telephone rang. It was Ted.

"They are on our wires and next door. They're spread out more. The leader is flying back and forth checking. Come on over and see."

John was torn between wanting to see the martins over at Ted's and be home in case dad's call came through. He couldn't leave now.

John started to set the table for supper.

The telephone rang.

Mother was upstairs and answered up there. John ran to the downstairs phone. "New York calling University 4-1424. Go ahead, New York," called the operator.

"Hello my J's. How are you all? Are you there?"

"Yes, dad," John answered.

"Yes, J.P.," said mother at the same time.

"Dad, the martins came today. Too many sat on the wire and busted it. But we got the trouble man here right away and he repaired it. Are you flying home tonight?"

60

"No, I have to make some reports in the office here but I'll be home tomorrow night. So glad I got you. I've been trying for two hours. It was those purple martins. Too many of us needed the wires at the same time!" Dad laughed as he hung up.

There was time for John to run over to Ted's and see the martins. There they all were, hundreds and hundreds, spread out on the wires back of three houses.

"It looks like a good convention," admitted John, "but I hope they come back to our house next year and spread out so no wires break."

Dad came home to his J's the next night. Janie hid behind mother at first, then walked right into his arms. John told all about his winter birds. He showed dad his bird record. Then he told about the martins' convention, how the wire broke and how it was repaired just in time for his call to come through.

The telephone rang. It was Uncle Jim and Grandmother. Uncle Jim was home, too. They would be over soon. The telephone rang again. It was Aunt Alice to say she'd be right over.

The telephone rang again. It was Ted to report that the martins were all gone.

The bird martins' convention was over.

The family Martin's reunion was just beginning.

All wires were up!

TELEPHONE WORKERS

Many people with many different kinds of jobs work together to keep our telephones working at all times.

Perhaps the telephone worker we are most familiar with is the *operator*. She helps us to place long distance calls that we cannot dial ourselves, she finds telephone numbers that are not listed in the books, and often helps trace people in times of emergency.

An operator is trained to handle the many calls that go through the large switchboards, and she learns to speak "with a smile in her voice."

The *service representative* takes care of any problems that we may have with our telephone service. If something is wrong with our phone she sends a telephone *repairman*, or *lineman*, to correct the trouble. If we move, she arranges to have a workman install a phone in our new home.

Men who have been educated in engineering, physics, and mathematics design new telephones and figure out ways to improve telephones and make the telephone system more efficient.